I love you!

A little book of love for you!

Juicylucy

Я

RAVETTE PU

First published in 2008 by
Ravette Publishing Ltd
Unit 3, Tristar Centre, Star Road
Partridge Green, West Sussex RH13 8RA

© 2007 Juicy Lucy Designs
All rights reserved.

www.juicylucydesigns.com

ISBN: 978-1-84161-298-0

I am so utterly in love with you. x

being with you makes me

slightly giddy..

.. You're the best thing since sliced bread..

Kiss me,

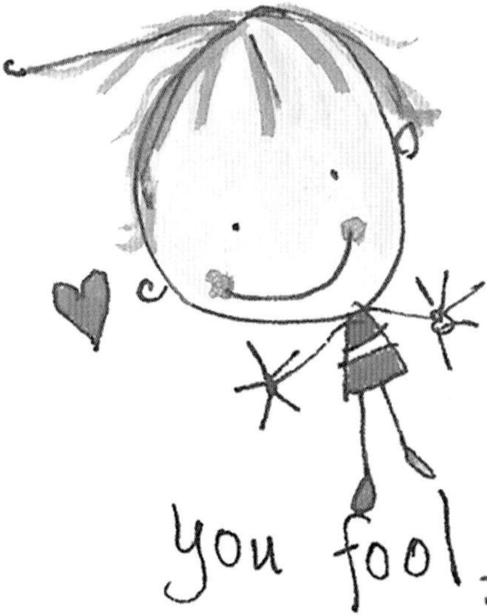

you fool

i love you more than...

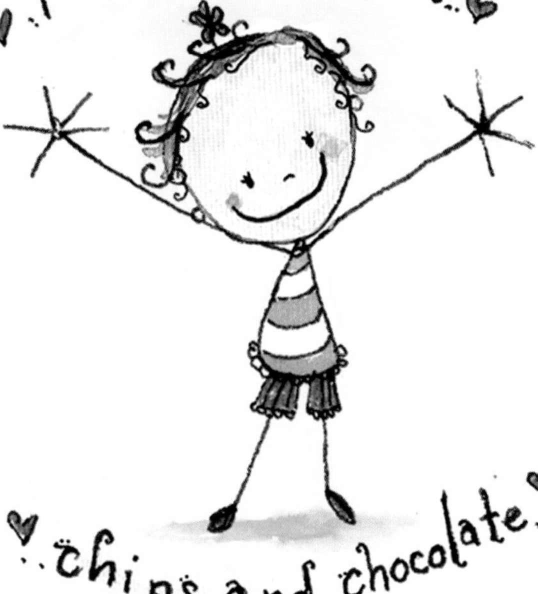

...chips and chocolate!

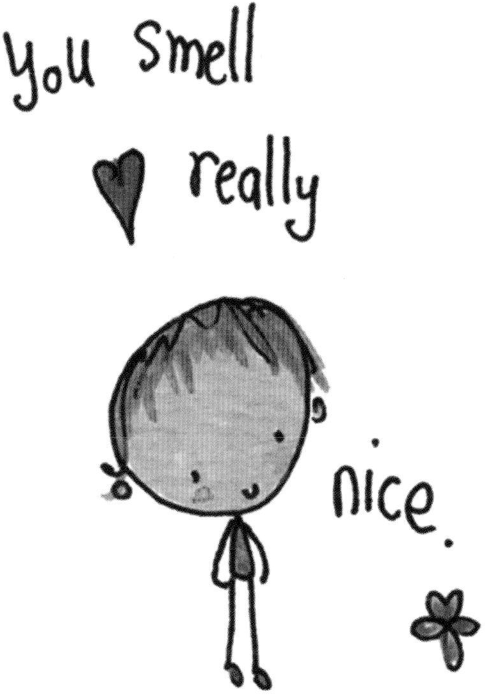
You smell
really
nice.

honey
bunny

You rather tickle my fancy ..

.Valentine..

..We make a great
team!

...thinking of you makes

my wings flutter...

I love you cheeky

monkey..

I love shogging you

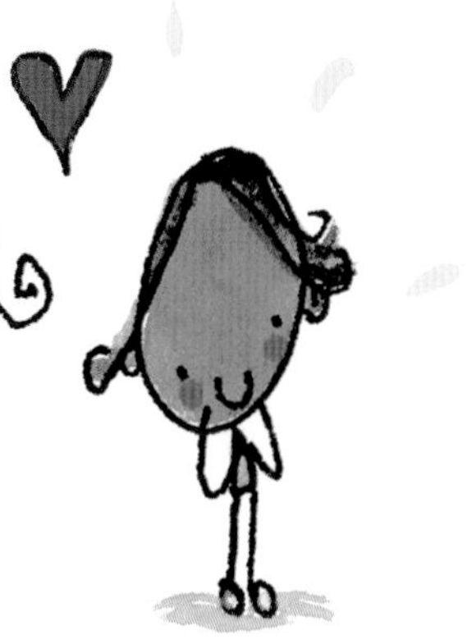

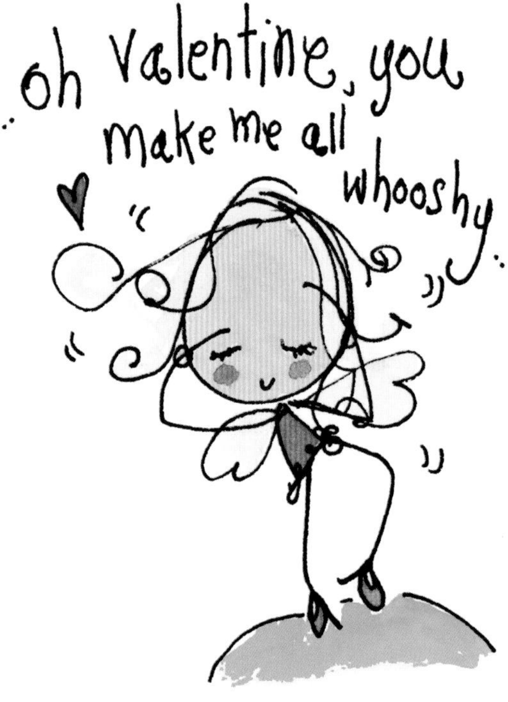
..oh valentine, you make me all whooshy..

I just really, really
really, really
really
really
really
love you x.

When you kiss
me it makes my
toes
wiggle. x

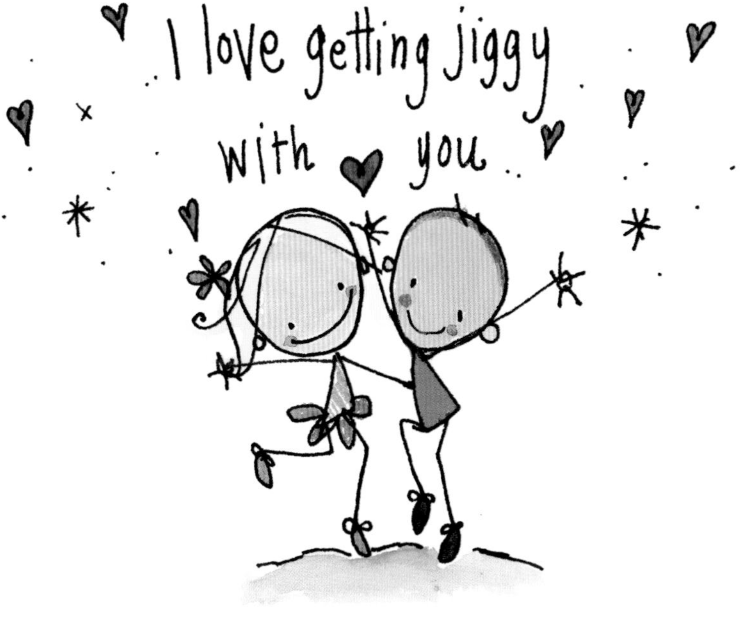
I love getting jiggy
with you

...I think I'm probably going to show you...

my knickers. x

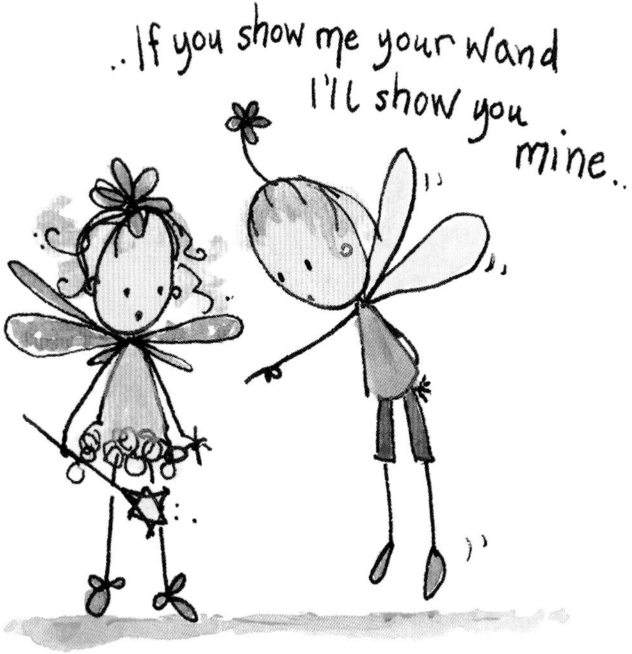
..If you show me your wand
I'll show you
mine..

..You're my boyfriend, my best friend..
and I love you !

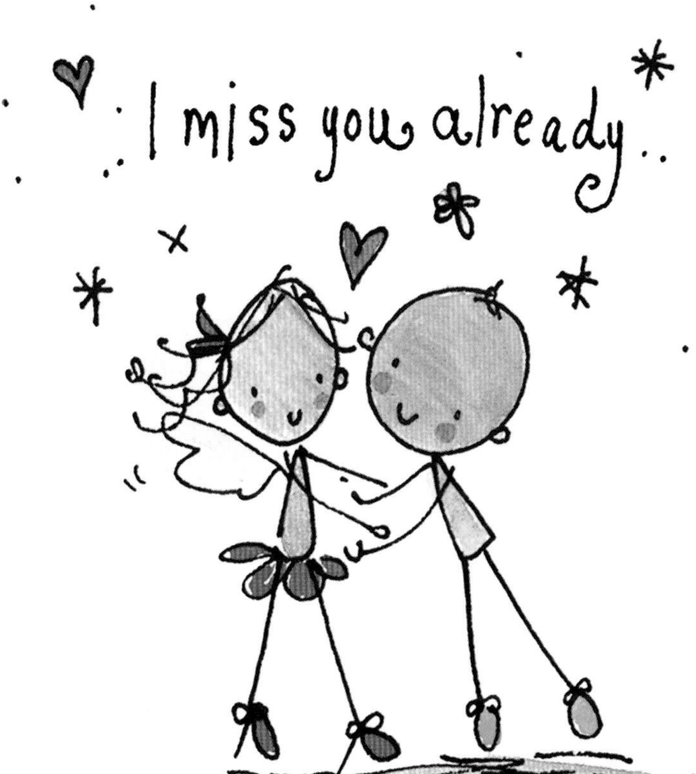
I miss you already

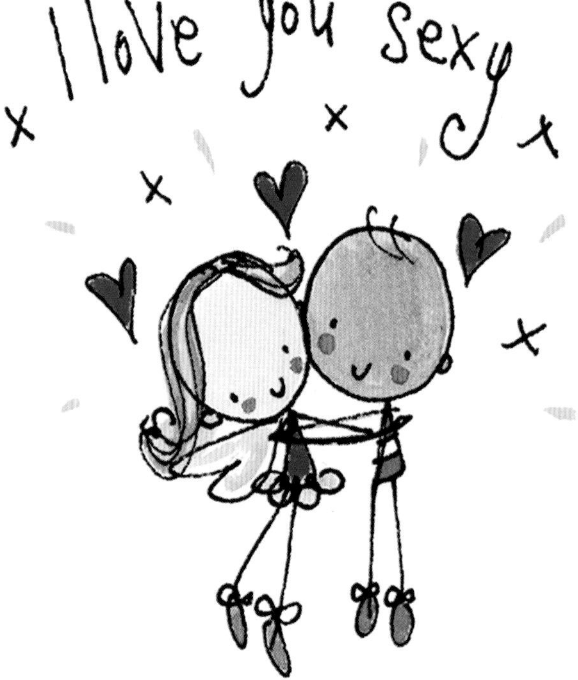
I love you sexy

You make such a difference in the world ❋

The little fairies think that you are
beautiful and special and kind!
They are thrilled that you have this book,
and want you to know that the lovely
people at Ravette have also published ...

	ISBN	Price
I love you mum	978-1-84161-300-0	£4.99
Let's be rudie nudies	978-1-84161-299-7	£4.99

HOW TO ORDER   Please send a cheque/postal order in £ sterling, made
                payable to 'Ravette Publishing' for the cover price of the
                books and allow the following for post & packaging ...

UK & BFPO   70p for the first book & 40p per book thereafter
Europe & Eire   £1.30 for the first book & 70p per book thereafter
Rest of the world £2.20 for the first book & £1.10 per book thereafter

RAVETTE PUBLISHING LTD

Unit 3 Tristar Centre, Star Road, Partridge Green, West Sussex RH13 8RA

Tel: 01403 711443   Fax: 01403 711554   Email: ravettepub@aol.com

Prices and availability are subject to change without prior notice.